TRAVEL BUG GOES TO ICELAND

WRITTEN BY
BOBBY BASIL

Copyright © 2019 Bobby Basil
All Rights Reserved.

No part of this publication may be reproduced or transmitted in any form or by any means except for your own personal use or for a book review, without the written permission from the author.

3 FREE BOOKS!

Go to travelbugkids.com!

I'm Travel Bug, and I love to travel!

I traveled very far
from my
home planet...

All the way
to Earth!

I want to
see and learn
EVERYTHING
about your planet!

On Earth,
I travel on a plane.

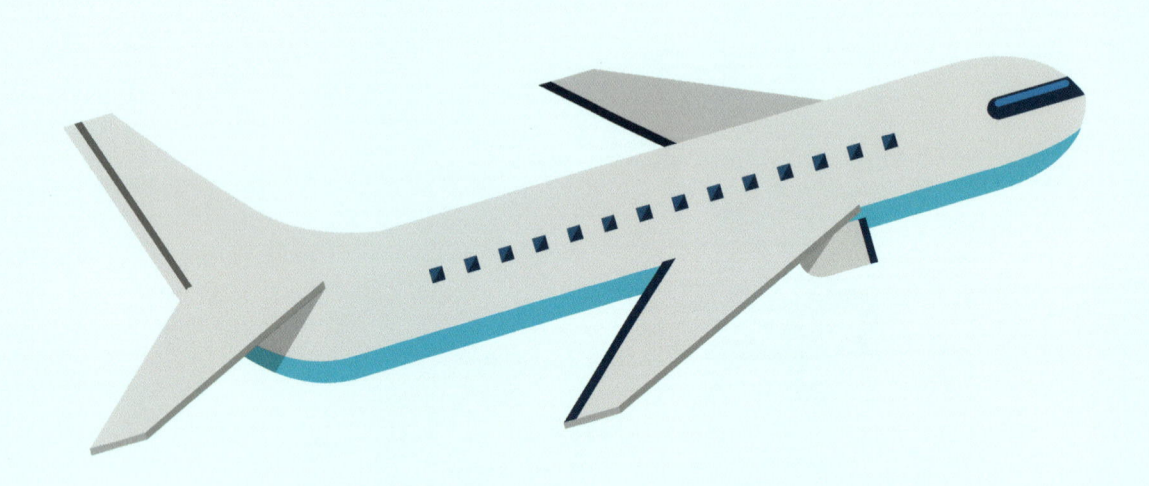

Planes can fly
all around
the world.

Today I am flying to Iceland!

That's a country in Europe.

This is what Iceland looks like on a map.

What do you think it looks like?

Iceland

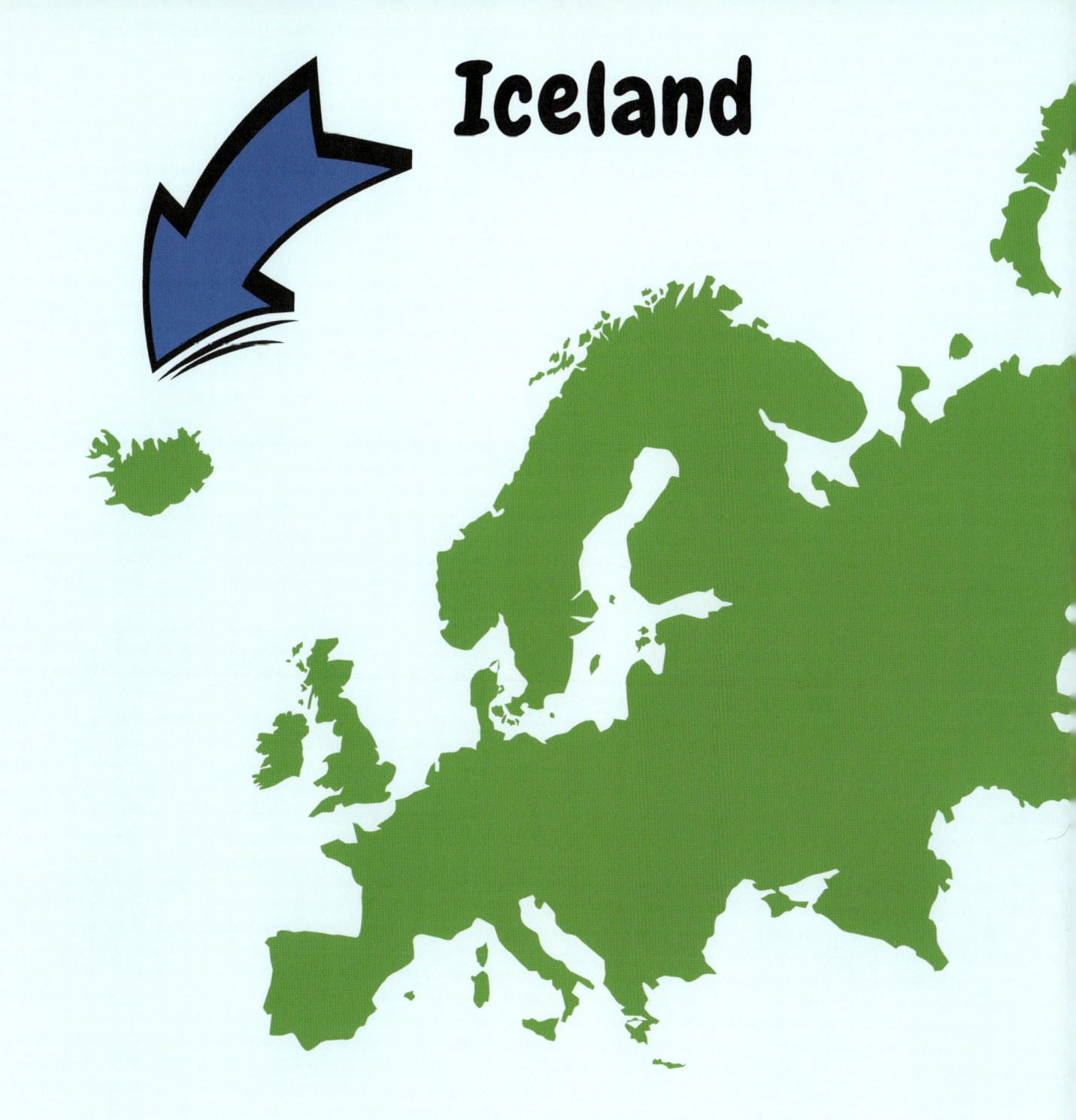

Iceland is in the northwest region of Europe.

Iceland is an island.

That means it has water on every side!

Iceland's island was created by Earth's tectonic plates pushing together.

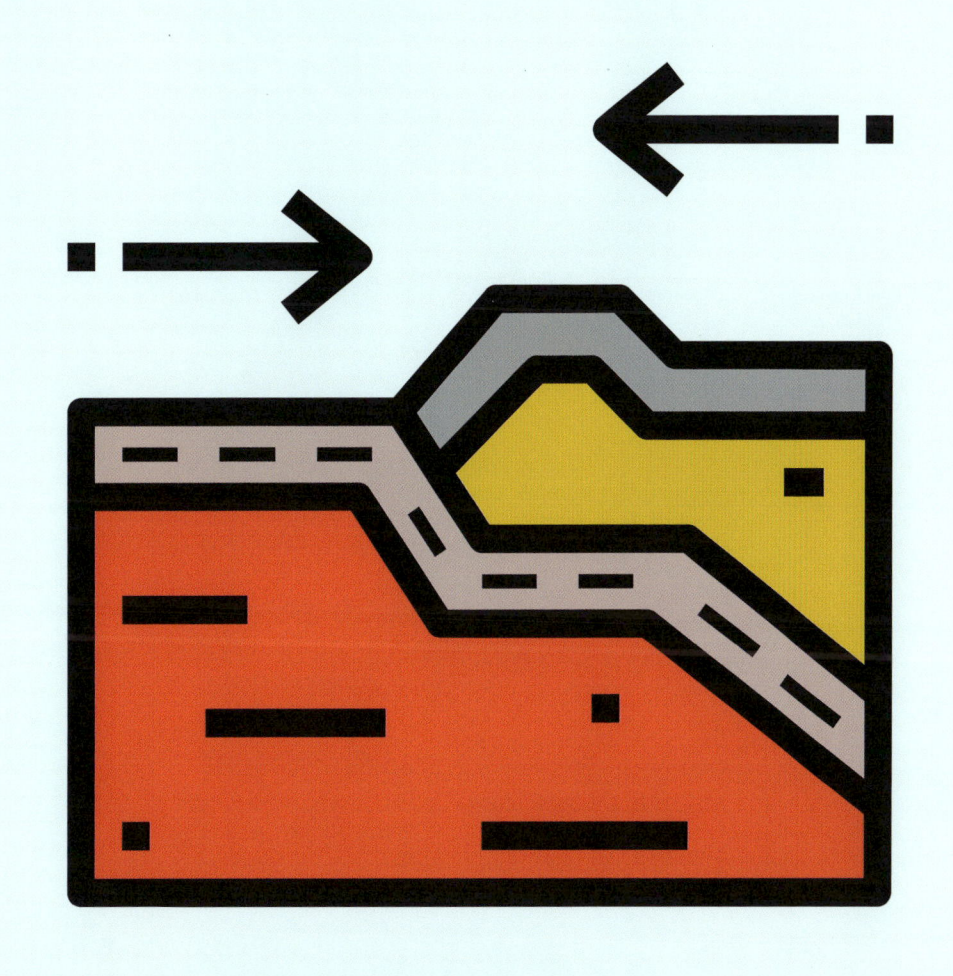

The tectonic plates pushing together created volcanoes!

Iceland has 130 volcanoes!

Iceland has geysers that shoot out water and steam!

Iceland also has beautiful waterfalls.

Iceland uses geysers and waterfalls to make energy.

This is called renewable energy.

Most people in Iceland speak Icelandic.

If you want to say hello in Icelandic, say "Halló"!

If you want to say thanks in Icelandic, say "Takk"!

In 874 AD, Vikings from Norway and the British Isles settled in Iceland.

Many people in Iceland are fishermen.

Have you fished before?

People in Iceland eat a lot of fish!

I like eating fish!

Iceland has glaciers because it is near the Arctic Circle.

It gets cold in Iceland during the winter!

I had a lot of fun in Iceland.

I can't wait to travel with you again!

PLEASE LEAVE A REVIEW ON AMAZON!

Your review will help other readers discover my books. Thank you!

Printed in Great Britain
by Amazon